LITTLE TIGER STARTS SCHOOL

Written by Sue Graves

Illustrated by Trevor Dunton

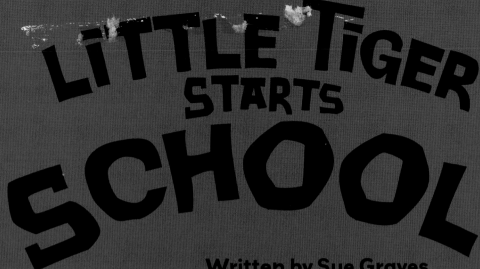

W
FRANKLIN WATTS
LONDON·SYDNEY

Little Tiger was starting school on Monday.
He was **very excited**. He had a pencil case
full of pencils. He had a new book bag, too.
Little Tiger was **very pleased**.

His sister said he would have his **own peg** at school. She said he had to hang his bag on it.

6

She said he had to put his pencil case in his
own tray. But Little Tiger was worried.
What if he couldn't find his peg or his tray?
what would he do?

Little Tiger went into the garden. He saw Tiger and Lion playing. They were having lots of fun. Little Tiger started to feel worried again. What if he didn't make any friends at school? **who would he play with** at playtime?

Then Little Tiger thought about Mrs Bear, his new teacher. He worried that she **might not be kind**. He worried that he **might not know what to do**.

Little Tiger thought school was **too scary**.
He didn't want to go at all!

Tiger and Lion saw Little Tiger.

They asked him what the matter was.

Little Tiger told them **all his worries**.

He said he didn't want to go to school.

He said school was too scary.

Lion and Tiger **listened carefully**.

Then Lion said Little Tiger didn't have to worry about anything. He said **everyone will help him** find his peg and his tray.

He only had to ask someone if he couldn't find something. Little Tiger felt **a bit better**.

Tiger said Mrs Bear was the kindest teacher ever!
She said that if Little Tiger **listened carefully**
to Mrs Bear, he would know what to do.

Little Tiger said he would listen very carefully to Mrs Bear. He felt **much better**.

Then Lion said lots of children felt
a bit worried when they started school.
He said he felt **very shy**. Little Tiger
was surprised. Lion wasn't shy at all!

Lion said luckily Hippo was **kind and helped** him. They became **good friends**. Little Tiger said he could help anyone who felt shy, too. Lion said that was a good idea. He said that was a good way to make new friends.

Soon it was the first day of the term.
Little Tiger got ready for school.
Mum and Dad said he looked very smart.
Dad **took a photo** of him.
Little Tiger was **very proud**.

At school, Little Tiger met Mrs Bear. She was very kind. She told everyone to **listen carefully**. Little Tiger remembered to listen very carefully. Mrs Bear said everyone had to try to find their pegs and hang up their bags.

Little Tiger quickly found his peg and hung up his bag. Mrs Bear **was pleased** that he had listened carefully.

But Little Cheetah **was worried**.

He couldn't find his peg.

He was **too shy** to ask Mrs Bear to help him.

Little Tiger remembered what Lion had said.

24

Little Tiger helped Little Cheetah find his peg …

… and his tray.

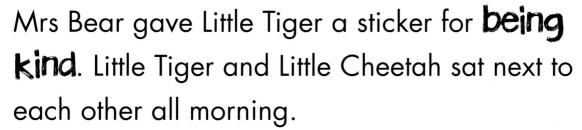

Mrs Bear gave Little Tiger a sticker for **being kind**. Little Tiger and Little Cheetah sat next to each other all morning.

At playtime, Tiger and Lion came to see if
Little Tiger was **all right**. But Little Tiger
was too busy playing with his new friend,
Little Cheetah.

Little Tiger said school was **brilliant**.

He said it wasn't scary at all.

Lion and Tiger laughed.

A note about sharing this book

The *Experiences Matter* series has been developed to provide a starting point for further discussion on how children might deal with new experiences. It provides opportunities to explore ways of developing coping strategies as they face new challenges. The series is set in the jungle with animal characters reflecting typical behaviour traits and attitudes often seen in young children.

Little Tiger Starts School
This story looks at some of the most common worries children have on first starting school. It also suggests strategies for overcoming their fears.

How to use the book
The book is designed for adults to share with either an individual child, or a group of children, and as a starting point for discussion.

The book also provides visual support and repeated words and phrases to build reading confidence.

Before reading the story
Choose a time to read when you and the children are relaxed and have time to share the story.

Spend time looking at the illustrations and talk about what the book might be about before reading it together.

Encourage children to employ a phonics first approach to tackling new words by sounding the words out.

After reading, talk about the book with the children:

- Talk about the story with the children. Ask them to retell the story in their own words. What happened first? What were Little Tiger's worries and concerns?

- Ask the children how Little Tiger felt by the end of the book. What things had he done to make him and others feel happier and more confident about starting school?

- Invite the children to recall their first days at school. What did they worry about? Did other people, especially older children, help them to settle in? Some schools set up 'buddies' from older age groups to help new pupils. If this is the case in your school, did the children find this system helpful?

Remind the children to listen carefully while others speak and to wait for their turn.

- Place the children into groups. Ask them to list all the things they worried about before starting school. Ask them to discuss amongst themselves how they resolved their worries.

- At the end of the session, invite a spokesperson from each group to read out their list to the others, together with their resolutions. Take the opportunity to remind the children always to look out for anyone who needs help at school and to be a good friend.

For Isabelle, William A, William G, George, Max, Emily,

Leo, Caspar, Felix, Tabitha, Phoebe, Harry and Libby –S.G.

Franklin Watts
First published in 2021 by
The Watts Publishing Group

Text © Franklin Watts 2021
Illustrations © Trevor Dunton 2021

Editor: Jackie Hamley
Designer: Cathryn Gilbert

A CIP catalogue record for this book is available
from the British Library.

ISBN 978 1 4451 7306 1 (hardback)
ISBN 978 1 4451 7309 2 (paperback)

Printed in China

Franklin Watts is a division of
Hachette Children's Books,
an Hachette UK company.
www.hachette.co.uk

MIX
Paper from
responsible sources
FSC
www.fsc.org
FSC® C104740